The People in the Rearview Mirror

Marlon K. Brown, Jr.

PublishAmerica
Baltimore

© 2005 by Marlon K. Brown, Jr.
All rights reserved. No part of this book may be reproduced, stored in a retrieval system or transmitted in any form or by any means without the prior written permission of the publishers, except by a reviewer who may quote brief passages in a review to be printed in a newspaper, magazine or journal.

First printing

ISBN: 1-4137-2517-1
PUBLISHED BY PUBLISHAMERICA, LLLP
www.publishamerica.com
Baltimore

Printed in the United States of America

Acknowledgments

This book is dedicated to my family and friends, especially my grandmother, Dolores Chambers. I have been extremely blessed to be surrounded by such wonderful people who have always encouraged and supported my writing, even when I was doubtful. I was lucky enough to be born into a family of colorful individuals who gave me a great foundation for becoming a man. I want to say thank you to my Godmother, Wanda Armstead, for the constant cheering and gentle smiles; to my Aunt Songy Turner (Tee) for being my first role model; and to my parents, Marlon and Cheryl Brown, for always guiding me to the next stage and making sure that I had the tools to get there. There is a special thanks to my grandmother for being my heart, my backbone, and my savior. And life would not be complete without the love of my siblings, Ashley and Bradley.

I must make mention of my oldest friend, Curtis LeBlanc. You were the first person to make me see I could do something special, and you never let me lose sight of it, even when I wanted to quit. And, I don't even have the words to express the gratitude I have for all the other posse members: Claudine, Nia, Saron, Keisha, Burt, Zeke, and Ron. You guys were my muses, and this story would have never been told without you. Among the list of individuals that helped me get there, I must say thank you to a man who has always had my back--Vincent Stokley. He clearly has angel wings hiding beneath that devilish exterior. And, in fact, I want to express my gratitude to the entire Stokley/Wheeler family, just for accepting a poor little college kid into your lives and making him feel like one of your own.

Finally, I have to show my appreciation to the Pruders: Harold and Omar. We have had each other our entire adult lives, and over the years we have taught each other to laugh at life and at ourselves. You guys have been there for the goods, bads, ups, downs, tears, snears, and uncontrollable laughter. You are genuine friends, and your friendship is priceless. You're angels and your friendship is something that I never expected at this point in my life, and I could never have asked for a better surprise. You will always be my family…always.

To everyone I have acknowledged, I want you to know that you have marked my life, and I love you all. Thank you for sharing the moments and being a part of my life.

The People in the Rearview Mirror

♦

The plane ride was rocky, and it had begun to rain. There were no cabs in sight, and Davis Williams was running low on cash. He had been waiting at the airport since two o'clock. It was now 2:30. Rodney was supposed to have been there when his plane touched down, but he wouldn't be Rodney if he wasn't late. Today had all the symptoms of being a bad day, except for the fact that Davis was back home. It had been over nineteen years since Davis had walked the streets of Little Rock, Arkansas, but it still felt like home.

By 2:45, Rodney had come cruising around to the passenger pick-up section in a 1981, powder blue Fairmont. Rodney had short, black, wavy hair, which he parted on the left and brushed to the right. He stood no taller than five-foot-seven and weighed only one hundred sixty-five pounds. His body was wrapped in an outdated grey suit, and he wore black and gold wire-framed glasses to match his black and gold class ring and diamond studded ID bracelet. As Rodney got out of the car, Davis yelled, "It's 'bout time yo slow ass got here."

"Well it's 'bout time you brought yo ass home," said Rodney with a huge smile across his face. The two hugged and loaded the bags into the trunk.

"I can't believe you still have this car. We used to ride around in this car over nineteen years ago."

"Yeah, I decided to keep the Blue Bird. I thought you'd get a kick out of seeing her. I gave her to my daughter for her eighteenth birthday. I keep the engine working, some new tires, a nice system, and she's as good as new. I try not to take her over 55 miles per hour now."

"Rod, you didn't drive over 45 when we were teenagers."

"'Cause driving slow saves gas and helps prevent accidents."

"You're still the same old Rod."

"Yup. Not much changed around here," continued Rodney, "except that Little Rocky is at Baines College now."

"Your kid is in college?"

"Yup. That's why I'm late. I wanted to go get the Blue Bird from her so I could surprise you."

"Matt's kid would probably be there with her," sighed Davis. "Have you heard from Matt lately?"

"Well, ugh...M-M-M-Matt's in the hospital."

"What happened?"

"He and Kennedy got into it the other night. She told him to leave, he wouldn't, she pulled out a gun and shot him. He should be out by tomorrow. He's gonna stay with Blake 'till he and Kennedy work this one out."

"Why don't they just get a divorce?" asked Davis.

"For what? Their marriage thrives on this. They do this all the time. Kennedy kicks him out, and he stays with Blake. They make up, then he goes home."

"I never could take crap like that. I would have just left, rather than go through all that."

"I know that's right. That boy ruined his whole life when he married Kennedy. They were still at Baines when Kennedy got pregnant. They did alright with the baby for a few years. Matt finished out one more semester before he flunked out, and Kennedy almost graduated."

"How old was the kid before he died?"

"Little Bobby was about four years old. It tore 'em up for a while."

"They never had anymore kids?"

"Nawh. Things was never the same after that child died. Kennedy started stayin' home and watching soap operas. She gained about seventy-five pounds, and Matt's still working at the garage. He goes down to the Sand Trap to get drunk. Every once in a while me or Blake have to go down there to get him 'cause he's drunk himself unconscious or started a fight or something."

"I can't believe this is what happened to the crew from Baines. We all had such high hopes. Me and Halle were gonna get together and write the Great American Novel, Blake was gonna deliver our kids, and you were gonna do our taxes."

"It's been a while since anybody's mentioned Halle's or Louis' names. Their little accident came as a shock to everyone."

"Their deaths were no accident. It was suicide. Right after it happened, Kennedy told me that they just didn't want to live anymore. People wanted to sugarcoat it and call it an accident, but you and I both know that they took their own lives. Halle overdosed, and Lou drove our grandmother's car into the lake," said Davis angrily. Rodney became relatively quiet and stayed that way for most of the drive home.

After a few minutes of silent tension, Rodney continued, "You and Lou were pretty close?"

"He was my cousin, Rod. And I never got to say goodbye. If I knew, when I left Little Rock, that I would never see him or Halle' again, I wouldn't have left the way I did."

"I warned you not to leave...you had everything here...friends, family."

"Jesus, Rod!" angrily interrupted Davis, "everything is so cut and dry with you. I know you didn't understand why I left, but I needed to make a life for me. I took a chance in my life, 'cause I was the only person that could make things happen for me."

"Okay man, I'm sorry. I know you made the right choice for you," said Rodney. Davis could tell his apology was phony. Rodney would agree with the devil if he thought it was the popular opinion.

"No, Rod, you don't understand. You had life handed to you. You work in your dad's bank, you went to the same college your dad went to because he was on the board of directors, and he told you to go to there. I don't even think you've ever had one single accomplishment that you got without your daddy spoonfeeding you through it. Can you name one thing, just one thing, that is all yours because you worked to get it?"

"Hey, I've worked for what I have."

"Ass-kissing doesn't count!" remarked Davis.

Silence fell over the car, and an air of awkwardness filled them both. "I'm sorry, Rod, but things have been rather hard for me. I'm just taking it out on you. I'm really sorry." Rodney quietly nodded his head and avoided eye contact with Davis.

"This is it," said Rodney as he drove into the driveway of a large, white two-story home. Parked in front of the Blue Bird was a white, luxury car and a dark-blue mini-van.

"This is your house, Rod?"

"Yup. My house. This is where me, Rocky and Jennifer live."

"You didn't say much about this wife of yours. You sure she won't mind me staying with you guys?"

"Nawh, man. You are one of my best friends and a member of the Baines Crew—if you need it and I got it, it's yours."

"Thanks, Man. I really appreciate this."

"No sweat," continued Rod, "but there is one thing you should know...Jennifer, my wife...she's white. Are you ok with that?"

"Of course I am."

"Well, my parents gave me a hard time about it at first, but they love her now. She's great. You'll see."

"Rodney, you are such a rebel," replied Davis sarcastically.

♦

By 4:15, Davis was settled into the guest room and was beginning to get used to his host and hostess' white-bread, suburban form of hospitality and humor. They were sitting in the den, enjoying cups of herbal-orange tea while Rodney told stories about the Baines Crew in college. They reminisced about the old-Friday-night-group dates and the way they all hung out in the library. Davis was eventually saved from more of Rodney's dry repetitive humor by the sound of two young people playfully trampling through the front door.

"Rocky!" called Rodney. "Come in here. There's someone I want you to meet."

"I have Noland with me!" she yelled back.

"That's Okay, he can come, too--for a small fee," laughed Rodney.

"I can't believe you call your daughter 'Rocky,'" said Davis.

"Well, Rodney's nickname was 'Rocky,'" said Jennifer. "So, when our first child was a girl, we named her Raquell—'Rocky' for short."

♦

The girl walked into the room, hand-in-hand with a young man. She almost looked Latin, with her long, wavy, black hair and tan skin. She was thin, like Jennifer, but had Rodney's small, dark eyes.

"Hi, Mr. and Mrs. Hall," said the boy, and he made a motion of 'Hello' toward Davis. Davis immediately noticed how handsome the boy was. He was five-foot-eight, with bright-brown skin, large, bright-brown eyes, and sandy-brown hair to match. He had broad shoulders with thick arms and a slight five o' clock shadow.

"This is Noland," said Rodney, "he's Rocky's boyfriend. Noland, this is a friend of mine, Mr. Davis Williams." Davis shook hands with the boy and noticed his small hands. The sound of a car horn rang in the distance.

"That's my Mom. We just came over to see if Rocky could have dinner at my house—we can drop her off later."

"Sure, but there's a one dollar late fee if you bring her back after ten," joked Rodney. Davis laughed, but he really didn't find it funny.

"Thank you, Daddy," said Rocky, as she kissed Rodney on the cheek, then ran upstairs to change clothes. Jennifer picked up the tea cups and headed into the kitchen. Davis sat there staring at Noland. Noland was extremely uncomfortable.

"Rod, this boy reminds me so much of Lou."

"Nawh, Lou was taller."

"Look at Noland's skin, his eyes, and his hair."

"Now that you mention it, he kinda looks like a young you."

"Me?!" squeeled Davis.

"Well, your dad and Lou's dad were twins, and the two of you basically had the same face." "Really, Honey, they could have passed for brothers," said Jennifer. "Only real difference was he was tall and thinner, and you were short and fat. Besides that, you two were identical." The car horn sounded again.

"That's my Mom again, Rocky, come on," yelled Noland.

"Yeah, Rocky, we don't want Noland's mom to have to come after ya'll," said Rodney.

"What's your last name, Noland?" asked Davis.

"It's Watson, Noland D. Watson."

"I once had a girlfriend named Watson, Paula Watson."

"Really?! That's my Mom's name."

"When's your birthday, Noland?"

"January 20th."

Davis could hear the sound of the front door closing, and felt anticipation from the click of her high heels against the tiled floor. This is what Davis needed. He needed to see her and make sure it was her. He held his breath a little--until he was sure it was Paula, the Paula he had loved and left over nineteen years ago. She was a short, thick woman with skin the color of creamy, milk chocolate. She still had wide, curvy hips and legs that most men only dream about. And, she still had a relatively small waist, which accented her perfect, hourglass figure.

The room had become uncomfortably quiet as Paula stood at the doorway like a goddess. She had keys in one hand and her hip in the other. She held everyone's attention in the palm of her hand. This was an ability she could activate by simply walking into a room. Her almond-shaped eyes pulled you in like a quiet storm, while her powerful voice demanded respect. Every word glided from her thick, auburn-painted lips.

"I thought I told you guys I was in a hurry--come on," she said, as she stormed into the den. She hadn't yet noticed Davis.

"Ma, I think this is a friend of yours."

"Who, Noland?" she asked. She was becoming irritated.

"Mr. Williams. He's right here." Paula was stunned. She was speechless. She couldn't believe he was here again. He still looked the same, except his forehead had grown slightly larger from his receding hairline, and he now wore a full beard and mustache, instead of his goatee.

"Davis," she gasped in disbelief.

"Hi, Paula. I bet you didn't expect to see me again."

"Oh, ya' got that right."

"Mr. Williams said you were old friends. Actually, he said you were his girlfriend."

"Yes, Noland, a long, long, long time ago," said Paula sternly.

"Okay, I'm ready," said Rocky who had just come bouncing down the stairs.

"Paula, I ah…," started Davis.

"You guys go get in the car," said Paula, handing Noland the keys.

"I don't really know what to say," continued Davis, "it's been so long and…"

"Davis, there really isn't anything for you to say. You didn't say anything nineteen years ago when you left in the middle of the night without a good-bye to anyone, so I don't expect you to say anything now."

"Paula, I was a kid! Can we at least talk?"

"I don't have anything to say," said Paula, as she turned to leave.

"Paula, really…let's be adults about this." Davis followed her into the next room.

"I was a kid too, Davis. But we all have to grow up eventually. We all learn to accept the responsibilities life gives us. And we deal with it." Davis grabbed her arm. She spun like a silent storm to face him. She shot an evil gaze down to his hand and then into his eyes. He leaned in close to her.

"I'm only going-off of how that boy looks and how you are treating me, but if I had to bet, I would say that that's my son. Is he Paula? Is Noland my son?"

"I didn't see you burping him, changing diapers, or paying for school. You weren't there when he lost his first tooth or graduated from high school. It takes more than a dick to make him yours, Davis."

"I didn't know, Paula. You didn't tell me you decided to have the baby. I was under the impression that we decided we were too young to be parents. I thought that you would have had it taken care of."

"I couldn't do it, Davis--I couldn't look myself in the eye if I had killed my baby."

"Well, how was I supposed to know if you didn't tell me?"

"I wouldn't have told you! I knew how you felt about kids, and I couldn't have ruined your life with my baby. If you would have stayed, I would have had the abortion."

"But, that's crazy. You're pissed 'cause I wasn't there, but you wouldn't have let me be there either."

"Look, Davis, I don't expect you to understand. Just like I don't expect you to be a part of Noland's life. When he was seven and wanted to know why he didn't have a daddy, it broke my heart. I never told him about you 'cause I didn't want him to ever feel unloved. Now, Noland is an intelligent, beautiful person, and I don't want his life to be upset by a father he never knew."

"But Paula, he's my son. I want him to know his father..."

"No, Davis! He's my child--mine. And, mine alone. Please just leave us alone. Good-bye. Bye Rodney, I'll have Rocky back by ten."

"O-o-o-o-k. See y-y-you at ten," stuttered Rodney. Paula quietly left, leaving Davis and Rodney alone. Davis found himself spellbound at the way her long, tan skirt gently swayed from the melodic motion of her hips.

"You knew about this?" asked Davis.

"S-s-s-s-sorta."

"You're stuttering. You only stutter when you're nervous or lying."

"Well, I always th-th-th-thought he was yours, b-b-b-but Paula n-n-n-never said anything t-t-t-to us."

"I have a son, Rodney. A son that is starved for the love of his father, and a daughter in Atlanta that wishes she didn't even know me."

"Why does your daughter feel that way?"

"Well, Kelly's fourteen and she blames me for what happened between me and Kristine."

"Is that why you're back here?"

"That's part of it. It's a long story, and frankly, I don't have the energy to go into it."

"That's alright, M-m-m-man. When you wanna t-t-t-talk about it, I'm here. Why don't you go get ready 'cause we gotta be at Slappy's in about an hour to meet Blake and Matt." Davis grabbed a quick shower and was ready in twenty minutes.

◆

They walked into Slappy's House of Blues. Davis spotted Blake and Matt from across the room. The Crew used to hang out at Slappy's on Friday nights. The layout of the place was basically the same. The mood was smoky and dark, and a few neon signs and dim lighting gave the place an eerie feeling. All the tables and bar stools were new, and the stage for local bands was now curtained off as a VIP area. Slappy's looked the same, and it all felt the same.

Blake Bennett was pushing forty, but he had the body of a twenty-five year old. He was gorgeous, an entrepreneur, and the consummate bachelor. At just the sight of Blake, it was obvious he put a lot of attention into his physique. When they were young Blake had flaunted the fact that he was saving himself for just the right woman. Now Blake was a fashion photographer who made bedmates of most of his subjects. Every once in a while, he enjoyed looking through his portfolio of photos to bask in every sweet conquest. When Davis spotted him, he was wearing a tan vest, no shirt, and tan slacks. He always wore dark sunglasses trimmed in gold. Blake loved to show off his muscularly-sculptured arms and the diamond-shaped tattoo on his left shoulder. He had a patch of silvery, grey hair on the front left side of his hair. It enhanced the shine of his chocolate-colored skin. This made him look particularly distinguished.

"Hey, Mr. Stranger," said Blake, as he and Davis shook hands and gave each other a half-hug. "Dang, you still got those small-ass hands."

"It's so nice to know that after all these years, we are still close enough for you to make comments on my dwarf-like qualities." Davis gave him a half-hearted smile and motioned to the bartender."Nothing like being with old friends and feeling like a freak." The three reunited friends took a seat at the corner of the bar. Blake's words made him think about Noland's small hands. He had psyched himself into forgetting Paula's biting words, but they kept replaying in his head. He wouldn't let himself get depressed all over again. He was back home, with all his "real" friends, and he was determined to have a good time.

"Took ya' long enough to show your face around here again..." continued Blake, "been a lot of changes since you left." Matt stumbled back from the bathroom. He gazed up at Davis and gave him an insincere 'Welcome Back.' Matt pulled up the seat at the bar beside Blake and reclaimed his beer. His once-dreamy, brown eyes were now bloodshot red.

"So the Golden-Boy returns," said Matt with a hint of animosity. "How long ya stayin' this time?"

"Not sure, Matt," answered Davis without emotion. "I'm here rather indefinitely for now."

"So," asked Blake, as he took a sip of his drink, "What's been goin' on?"

"I suppose you guys know this already, but I just found out that I have a son." Blake took a deep breath and swallowed down at his drink. Everyone else remained quiet. "Why didn't any of you guys tell me about Noland?"

"None of us really knew what was going on between you and Paula," said Blake. "You took off without a word, a few months later she turns up pregnant, then there was the thing with Lou and Halle. We all figured you knew, and it was none of our business. In fact, we thought that was why you left. Look, Noland's a good boy. He and Paula take real good care of each other. He's an honor student over at Baines College. Things really didn't turn out all that bad."

"That depends on whose eyes you're looking from. I just can't believe everything is so much different than the way we planned it. Blake, you were gonna be a doctor and you and Halle were supposed to get married."

"You always did plan too much, Davis. I wanted to be a doctor, but I 'm a photographer, and I'm a damn good photographer. I really like my life."

"Why didn't you ever settle down and have kids?"

"'Cause they won't be Halle's kids. I let the woman I loved slip through my fingers, and now it's too late. Love like that doesn't happen twice."

"Dude, that was almost twenty years ago. You are still hung up on her. Even I found someone to love," said Rodney.

"As usual, you don't get it, Rod. I tried being with other girls, but it's just not the same. None of them felt right. But, like I said, I like my life. Just 'cause I don't come home to the same person every night does not mean that I'm not happy."

"Are you happy, Blake?" asked Davis.

"I'm content. We can't change the past. We can only make the best of what we have now."

"Ain't that the truth," chimed in Matt.

"So, you think if I had been here when she was thinking about doing it, maybe I could have stopped her?" asked Davis.

"It's not your fault, Davis. I made her feel like I didn't really love her--she never would have done it. Trust me...beating yourself up over this is not the answer...I've done that for years, and it's gotten me nowhere. Don't get me wrong—I'm financially stable. I'm in great shape."

"But, you're not happy."

"Maybe I'm not jumping for joy. The truth is I'm lonely. I know I didn't make her take those pills, and this all happened so long ago that it shouldn't matter anymore, but I just can't bring myself to love another woman like I love Halle."

"You can't keep blaming yourself either, Blake."

"I know we can't keep living in the past, but sometimes it just hurts so much. I guess I never really dealt with it. I kinda stuck it in the back of my mind. When you left, I didn't have anyone to hold my really-deep conversations with. Whenever I got really serious, it either scared people away or it went right over their heads. I guess seeing you just stirred up all those old emotions that I had buried deep inside."

"It's okay, Man. I'm here now."

"Guys, what Halle and Lou did, they did to themselves and that's nobody else's fault but theirs. We're supposed to be happy—Davis is finally back home," said Rodney.

"So, here's to the future, to the past, and to now," said Blake, as they raised their drinks and water glasses for a toast. "Especially the now."

"So, if you guys are finished with your little love-fest of memories, I wanna know what made you come back here?" slurred Matt.

"Well, it's a long story."

"We got time," said Rodney.

"Looking back, it seems like I did everything right…but, it all turned out wrong. After I left for Atlanta, I went to school on a scholarship for the next three years at the University of Atlanta. I met Kristie, and two years after graduation, we were married. I got a job, we had Kelly, and the money started rolling in. We bought a big, beautiful home and became the ideal little family. Our lives were perfect, until Kristie decided being the wife of a journalist wasn't good enough. After a while, things just started falling apart. She and I would fight every night, and eventually we just grew apart. Last week I came home and my house was practically empty. Kristie and Kelly had moved out, and one of the few things they left was my freshman yearbook from Baines. There I was sitting on the bare floor of my now-empty den, thumbing through this book that I hadn't touched in years. I ran across this picture of the Crew sitting in the library. It made me start thinking about you guys and how close we were. The Crew was my family and my support. I guess I'm here because I need to feel that support. One minute I'm the happiest guy on earth, the next I'm sitting in an empty house wondering what the hell I'm supposed to do now. When I was a kid, I had planned on being the ideal husband and father, and I was, or at least, I thought I was. I had it all, but now I got jack shit."

"You got too comfortable, Man," said Blake, "you gotta be ready to accept change when it happens."

"I know, I just didn't expect this much of a change from life. I guess somebody upstairs wanted to snap my ass back into reality. Make me see that I still lived on earth with the other mortals."

"You wanna see change," slurred Matt in his drunken tone, "check this out." He pulled a picture of Kennedy from his wallet. She now looked much older, and a hackneyed expression was painted all over her face. She was smiling, but her eyes weren't happy anymore. Her hair had grown out to the point where her black roots were at ear level in her shoulder-length, brown-dyed hair. Her hips, chest, and stomach were much bigger. "I guess she's not something you want anymore, huh?"

"I never wanted Kennedy, Matt. She was my friend. In fact, she was Paula's best friend. Most of our conversations were about Paula and you." Davis' voice was gradually becoming louder.

"Sure, Dave—I know better than that. My whole life you have been competing with me, and you were always the winner. Finally, I had something. The pretty girl actually wanted me. Then you and your cousin Lou tried to take that away from me. But cha couldn't. Kennedy was mine. But, I guess you still won, 'cause Kennedy ain't beautiful no more, she ain't rich, and she ain't happy. The only good part about the whole thing is that Lou never got her either. Too bad the fool had to kill himself over it."

"You're a sick bastard, Matt."

"I know I ain't shit in your eyes. I don't have a big, fancy house in Atlanta, or degrees to hang over my fireplace. Hell, I don't even have a fireplace, but I'm still here trying to survive. I didn't give up on my family and run away."

"Don't try to make us feel bad about you screwing up your life."

"What could I accomplish? Tell me Davis, what was I supposed to do? When everything crumbled, where were you? Being smart didn't come naturally to me like it did to you. After you left, I didn't care about Baines College anymore. I had a family to support and Baines wasn't doin' shit for me."

"I can't believe you're trying to blame your screwed up life on me."

"Ya know what, Davis Williams...you can go to hell, or wherever the hell you went. You're such a selfish bastard-- you never thought about how your leaving affected us," said Matt. His knees were wobbly, and his head was spinning.

"Alright, time to go," said Blake as he put Matt's arm around his shoulder and dragged him to the car. "He's just an angry drunk—don't listen to him."

"I know. I'll see you guys later," said Davis, "maybe we can do this again when Matt's sober.

"We'll see, Davis. Just gimme a call. Rodney's got the number." Blake took a moment to situate Matt on his shoulder. "Well, alright, Man. I'll see you later. And, Davis, I'm glad you're home."

"Thanks, Blake."

♦

On the way home, Matt's words kept repeating in Davis' mind. Maybe this was his fault. Maybe it was karma coming back. His leaving seemed to ruin their lives, and now it was his turn to watch his life crumble. Maybe Matt was right about Davis being selfish. When he had left, it had been purely out of his own greed.

That night, he lay in bed thinking about his kids, his wife, his friends, and Paula. Davis went to his bags and pulled out a bottle of small, orange pills. He took a handful and swallowed them without water. He took another handful and gulped those down, too. Davis Williams hated himself for the things he had done in his life. His world had come crumbling down around him, and his light of hope had gone out. Davis didn't care what tomorrow would bring, as long as he didn't have to face it.

After spending a night of tossing and turning, trapped by the walls of depression, he awoke to the sound of knocking. He was disoriented. The room was dark and unfamiliar. The knocking was like pounding hammers on his temples. Luckily, he found the window and opened it. Rod was standing outside. He climbed into the room and asked if Davis was ready to go.

"What are you talkin' about Rod? It's the middle of the night. Where are we going?"

"Y-y-you told me to be at your house at 10:00, and it's now 10:15. We have to hurry if we are gonna make the 11:45 flight."

"What flight?!" asked Davis angrily. He still hadn't gained his bearings. Then his sight began to clear, and he noticed Rod's mane of soft, jet-black curls of hair that garnished his head. He was wearing contact lenses and a green-and-white-striped shirt with green jeans. Davis remembered that being the last thing he saw Rodney wear before he left 19 years ago. Rodney's apparent youth made Davis realize he was either dreaming or somehow back in time. Davis was being given the opportunity to fix the lives of his friends—lives that he felt he had destroyed.

"Rod, how old are you?" asked Davis.

"I'm nineteen. What's wrong with you?"

"Jesus, Rod!" he screamed.

"Shhh, Man, you're gonna wake up Louis. I thought we were supposed to keep all this hush- hush."

"We are! I mean, we were…I'm not goin', Rod. I'm not doin' it!" said Davis excitedly. "Wait a minute...you said Lou...Lou is here?" It was all becoming clear. Davis realized that he was in the house he grew up in. He lived there with Lou, Lou's mom, and their grandmother. This was the home he was raised in, and the home he ran away from. This was the home that took him in as a baby when his own parents deserted him at birth.

Davis clicked the light on, and on the other side of the room, there was a bed containing the six-foot-one, two-hundred-pound mass of man called 'Lou.' Louis jumped from the light. He raised his head and opened his gentle brown eyes. They were momentarily red. "What the hell are you doing?" asked Lou in a deep, irritated tone. Davis ran over to Lou's bed, jumped on top of him, then tightly wrapped his arms around Lou's thick body.

"Lou, it's been nineteen years, and you're still the same."

"Boy, I saw you an hour ago when we went to bed," said Lou as he pushed Davis off.

"Lou, ya just don't know," said Davis. Rodney was standing there with a huge smile on his face.

"Bruh, you d-d-don't know how glad I am that y-y-you're not going."

"Where ya goin?" asked Louis.

"Nowhere. I'm stayin' right here in Little Rock."

"Bull!" said Lou, "now tell me where you were going."

"I was gonna take the scholarship at University of Atlanta."

"So, you were just gonna leave and not tell anybody…"

"It doesn't matter. I'm not going."

"I don't know, and I don't care. What I do know is you're much better off here," added Rodney.

"But you always wanted to go away."

"Lou, it doesn't matter anymore. I'm not going."

"Look ya'll, I had to beg m-m-my parents to let me out of the h-h-house this late," said Rodney "and I don't have to be home 'till 3:00, so let's not just sit around here. I wanna go somewhere."

Davis' first thought was to go see Kennedy. Kennedy, aside from Louis, was his best friend. They could talk about almost anything. There was nothing Kennedy didn't know about Davis. Both Matt and Paula had problems with the fact that Kennedy and Davis were so close. Louis was about the only other person that understood a man and a women being friends--just friends. Davis was in love with Paula, but he loved Kennedy. She would listen to him and advise him. She also wasn't afraid to tell him when he was being an ass. Considering what Kennedy would go through within the next few years, he really needed to see her.

"Look, Rod, I need to pass by Kennedy's house," said Davis excitedly.

"Why is it you need to see my girlfriend now?" asked Louis.

"Kennedy is not your girlfriend."

"How would you know, Rod?"

"Because you sat in the Blue Bird last Friday night and cried to me and Davis about how Kennedy needed her space. Look at you. You're craving her."

"Boy, please," said Lou, who was slightly irritated, "but, if ya'll are going over there, I'm coming."

"Okay, just put some clothes on and let's go."

The three of them snuck out the window and drove about four miles to Kennedy's house. Unfortunately, Kennedy was not there. Halle told them that she had gone to the lake with Matt. Davis had forgotten that Halle was Kennedy's sister. Obviously, Blake had not broken the news to her yet because she still sounded happy. It was nice for Davis to see Halle again. In fact, stopping her suicide would be his next mission.

The guys headed up to the lake. They spotted Matt's station wagon sitting quietly near the edge of the water.

"I guess your girlfriend is having a good time in Matt's car," joked Rod.

"Don't say that shit no more," angrily commented Lou. They parked about twenty feet from Matt's car.

"You guys stay here. I'm gonna go find Kennedy—then we can leave." Davis approached the car apprehensively. After all, he didn't know what was going on in that car, but he had an idea. Davis remembered what it was like to grab a quickie on the lake. When he looked in the window, he saw Kennedy and Matt's naked bodies nestled against each other. It was quickie time. Luckily, their private parts were covered by a thin blanket. They had seemingly fallen asleep watching the stars. Their clothes were scattered across the back seat. Davis noticed how beautiful Kennedy was while she slept. Her sexy, deep-set eyes were closed, and her long, wild, sandy-brown hair was covering a part of her left cheek. He also noticed how much nicer Matt looked before his body became worn and bloated from the years of hard work and alcohol abuse.

Davis' first reaction was to walk back to the car and hope Louis wouldn't ask too many questions. The last thing he needed was for Louis to see this. Unfortunately, when he turned around, Louis was standing right behind him. Kennedy opened her eyes. Everyone was speechless. Louis stormed away and Davis followed.

"Bruh, you are so much better off without her," said Davis. He was trying to catch Louis before he exploded.

"I can't believe she did this to me."

"Well, you know she's not really cheating on you, 'cause you're technically not her boyfriend."

"But, why did she do it with him?" asked Louis. His voice was cracking, and his hands began to shake."Where am I gonna find somebody else like her?"

"Lou, she's not worth it, Man."

"This just hurts so much, Davis. It's killing me, man. I love her." Just then, Kennedy darted from the back of the station wagon. She had managed to put her jeans and tank top back on.

"Lou, wait," she called. She caught them midway between the cars. "I'm sorry, Lou. I didn't mean for you to see this."

"Is this why you wanted your space? So you could screw Matt?"

"Lou, it's not just a crush between me and Matt. I fell in love with Matt. And, you can't always control who you fall in love with."

"Yeah. Save it, Kennedy," said Lou. He angrily walked back to the car and slammed the car door.

"Davis, what are ya'll doing out here?"

"I really needed to talk to you, but this really isn't a good time."

"No shit, Sherlock!"

"You know, he really cares for you, Kennedy."

"I know, and I can't stop him from feeling that way. That's his problem, and right now, I really need to be with Matt."

"If you and Matt keep this up, you could end up pregnant."

"It's a little late for a lecture," said Kennedy.

"I'm serious, Kennedy!" yelled Davis.

"So am I!"

"Are you saying you're pregnant now?"

"Yeah, I found out last week. That's why I broke it off with Lou. Matt said he would marry me."

"Jesus, Kennedy! That's gonna kill Lou," exclaimed Davis. "Why would you mess around with two men at the same time?"

"You know, I wasn't looking for a husband. I just wanted to have some fun with them. I didn't plan this, but things got serious with me and Matt. Then I found out I was pregnant, and I didn't see any reason to lead Lou on."

"So, I'm too late for you and Matt."

"What are you talking about?"

"Nothing. You just make sure you know what you're doing by marrying Matt. I won't try to stop you...'cause I know you...and I know how you feel about people telling you what to do. Just make sure this is who you want to wake up next to for the rest of your life." Louis stretched his head out of the car window and urged Davis to hurry. Davis noticed that Matt had also awakened and was standing beside the car. He hadn't bothered to put his shirt back on, but he was wearing a faded pair of denim, blue jeans and a pissed-off expression.

"Think you could finish this conversation some other time?!" yelled Matt. Davis kissed Kennedy on the cheek, then dashed into the back seat of the Blue Bird.

♦

Lou sat quietly, facing the window as they drove home. "It does get better," said Davis.

"Really?" replied Lou with a dry tone of sarcasm. He hadn't bothered to turn his head from the window.

"Life, it gets better. I know you feel like shit now, but no girl is worth losing your life over."

"Do you really think I would kill myself over Kennedy? Believe me, I'm way past that stage. But that doesn't mean I wouldn't like to crawl up into a little ball and die." Davis noticed that they were passing through Paula's old neighborhood.

"Rod, I need to stop at Paula's."

"It's after 2:00 in the morning, and I-I-I-I gotta be home by th-th-th-three."

"I promise I will only be five minutes."

"Bruh, I-I-I don't know."

"Please, Rodney. I really need to see her."

Paula lived on the corner of her block, so that made it easy for Davis to sneak around the back where Paula's bedroom was. He knocked on her window, and almost immediately, she poked her head out of the window.

"Boy, what are you doin'? It's two-something in the morning!"

"Paula, I know but I had to come. I had to tell you that I love you." She was wearing an oversized, pink nightshirt and a blue-and-white scarf to cover her short, dark brown hair. She wasn't wearing any make-up, but to Davis, she was still the most gorgeous thing he had ever seen.

"You're at my window at two in the morning just to say you love me? Do you realize that you spent yesterday pointing out every reason why we should not be a couple," she said angrily.

"Paula, what are you talking about?"

"I'm talking about the big fight we had at Baines yesterday. You made one of your comments, I got mad, you confronted me about my attitude, you told all our friends that we were splitting up because you were tired of my shit. Need I go on?" Her voice was becoming a whirlwind of tension, building with each word that flew from her rich, powerful lips.

"I did? Well, I didn't mean it!"

"What about the other shit about our relationship being a 'well-rehearsed dance of arguments,' and you being 'tired of dancing?'"

"I didn't mean that, either. I would dance with you forever if you still wanted me to."

"You also said that we were too young to be this serious."

"Girl, you know I'm young and stupid. Why would you listen to me?" joked Davis. Just then, Rodney beeped the car horn.

"Damn," he said as he glanced down at his watch, " I have to go."

Paula was blushing. His words made her feel like a queen, and her smile let him know that all was forgiven. "This isn't the way I wanted to tell you this. But if you love me the way you say you do, and if all the things you are saying right now are true, then we have to talk and it's a really big deal. I'm…I'm…"

"Shhh, Paula," he whispered as he slid his pointer finger over his lips, "just know that I love you more than anything on earth. And, I trust that you'll do the right thing. We can get through anything together. I already know the answer, but would you promise me that you will never leave me?"

"Oh, Davis," she said as she covered her mouth. "You don't know how good it feels to hear you say that. I really thought I had lost you this time. You know I would never leave you."

"Don't worry. I ain't going nowhere. Trust me." Davis smiled, gave her a quick peck on the cheek, and dashed across her yard, where he disappeared into the back seat of the Blue Bird.

♦

The ride home was extremely quiet. Davis and Lou climbed back into their bedroom and went to sleep without another word. For Davis, the morning came too soon. He was awakened by Louis, who was already half-dressed.

"What are you doin' up so early—I thought we were on summer vacation."

"Boy, we gotta go to work. Remember our jobs…at Baines…in the library. Any of this ringing a bell to you?" Lou was joking, but he still looked depressed.

"How you feeling about last night? You wanna talk?"

"Naah, I'm alright, but I don't think I'm going with you and Rod on Crew night."

"Crew night? That's right, it's Friday. Crew night."

"I don't think I can take running into Kennedy and Matt together," he sighed. "You better get up, you gonna make us late."

"Believe me, being late is the least of our problems."

♦

Davis and Louis went to work stocking books in the library, but they avoided Matt, who also worked there. Davis noticed that the ordinarily jovial Lou was being very quiet and withdrawn. He would occasionally stop working and slip into a deep, focused stare. His eyes became glassy, and his face would go blank. It was as if he was momentarily transported to another world in the deepest recesses of his mind, where happiness was the theme, and Kennedy was his. Davis knew he was too late to really change anything for Kennedy, but he was determined to keep Louis and Halle from killing themselves.

Their suicides were two, totally isolated and unrelated events that coincidentally occurred on the same night. Davis wasn't sure how, but he would have to keep tabs on two different people, in different places, at the same time. Lou was certainly acting like a prime candidate for suicide, but Davis figured as long as he didn't leave his side, he could hold on to him. Halle, on the other hand, lived on the other side of town.

After work, Davis borrowed his grandmother's car and headed across town to talk to Kennedy. He figured he could blow off some steam and keep an eye on Halle at the same time. Unfortunately, Kennedy was out somewhere with Matt, and he didn't really feel like looking for her. Though Kennedy was gone, he did find Halle. She didn't look too disturbed, so he concluded that whatever it was that drove her to the pills hadn't occurred yet. Halle seemed so happy right now, with her beautiful, brown eyes and a joyfully innocent smile. They sat and talked for a while. Halle never got tired of talking about Blake, and right now he seemed to be the nucleus of her life. Just before he left, he assured her that if she ever needed anything or anyone to talk to, he was there. She gave him a slightly confused glance, said "Okay," and watched him drive off.

Davis went back home. He hoped he could convince Louis to go out and cheer up a bit. This was supposed to be Crew Night, but everybody else seemed to have made other plans. He could not take an entire night of Rodney's dry humor alone. To his surprise, Lou wasn't there. Lou claimed he needed to get some fresh air, so he borrowed his mom's car. Davis figured he would only be gone for a few minutes, and what could happen to Lou in that short a time?

Slowly, everything was falling apart, and nothing was working out the way he expected. He had no idea where Louis was, and he was starting to get worried. Maybe Lou really did just need some time alone to work this out for himself. About an hour later, Davis dozed off in front of the television. At about 11:30, the phone rang. It was Halle, and she was crying. *This is it*, he thought.

"He broke up with me," she said between sobs and sniffs.

"Okay, Halle, calm down and tell me what happened."

"He said that he was having some problems and having a girlfriend was just adding to it–but, that's a lie! I could tell it was a lie…" Her word were getting lost in the sobs.

"Slow down, Halle. Start at the beginning, and tell me what you're talking about."

"Okay. The other night we were alone at his house. We were making out, and we were going further than we ever had before. I was ready to...you know. I wanted to go all the way, but he wouldn't." Her voice was cracking from the crying, and some of her words were still very indistinguishable. "He thinks I'm a slut, and who wants a slut for a girlfriend?"

"Halle, I don't think it's that. You can't blame yourself for this. If he leaves you, it's his loss."

"No," she continued through the sobs. "We talked about this and we agreed to wait until marriage for sex, but I got wrapped up in the moment, and I pressured him."

"Halle, this is not your fault. My grandmother used to say…I mean my grandmother says everything happens for a reason and sometimes you gotta have a little conversation with God and ask him why they're happening. Eventually, he'll tell ya."

"You know, I don't think I have ever heard you mention God before."

"I'm looking at things a little differently these days and I realize that I should have spent a lot more time listening to my grandmother." Halle sighed and Davis could hear the sound of the doorbell ring in the background. She excused herself and went to answer it. Davis could hear a male voice in the background. He hoped it was Blake coming back to make up. Halle returned to the phone. She told Davis that she would call him back, and then she hung up.

That was rather easy, he thought. *All I had to do was talk to Halle for five minutes to keep her from killing herself. She just needed somebody until Blake came to his senses.* Davis went back to sleep for about an hour. He woke again to find Lou still not home. This was really starting to scare him. He took the car and drove back up around the lake. He thought Lou may have gone there looking for Kennedy, but there was no sign of him, Kennedy or Matt. He drove to Kennedy's house thinking that maybe she was home, or maybe she had run into Lou.

When Davis got there, Matt's car was outside. Kennedy answered the door.

"I thought you were Halle," she said. Davis knew something was wrong by the worried look on her face and the frustrated tone in her voice.

"Where is Halle?" asked Davis. Kennedy hesitated then explained that Louis was there when she and Matt returned home. Lou got upset, they exchanged insults, then he stormed out. Halle followed him, but not without taking the time to tell Kennedy how much of a bitch she was for playing with his emotions. That was close to three hours ago, and no one had heard from them since. Just then, Matt came from the other room with a bunch of damp towels in one hand, and a glass of water in the other.

"I just got Paula to go to sleep, but I'm gonna keep the compresses on her head until the fever stops," he said before he realized Davis was in the room.

"Paula's here?"

"Yeah, but she's asleep."

"What's wrong with her, Kennedy, why is she here? Is she sick?"

"Davis, you and I have always been straight with each other, and you know Paula has been my best friend for years, so I don't feel right being the one to tell you this, but you need to know."

"Kennedy, what is it?"

"Me and Matt took Paula to the clinic. She had an abortion today. The doctor says she'll be kinda sick for a few days, so I'll take care of her. But she'll be alright."

"Why, Kennedy? Why did she do this?"

"'Cause she knew how you felt about becoming a parent at nineteen years old. She knew about all the plans you had for your life and how having a baby would ruin it for you."

"I don't believe this," said Davis.

"Why don't you go on home, get some rest. If Lou comes back here, I'll tell him you're looking for him. She'll be fine by Sunday, okay? Me and Matt will bring her home, and then you two can talk this all out."

"I wanna see her!"

"Davis, she's so drugged-up, she won't know you from Adam. Let her sleep and you'll see her on Sunday."

♦

Everything was going wrong for Davis. Nothing was flowing according to his plan. The one thing he still counted on was that Lou and Halle were both steered away from death's path.

Meanwhile, on a secluded spot of the lake, Louis and Halle sat in his mom's dark blue, town car talking under the moonlight, listening to the crickets chirp and the sound of the waves brush against the shore.

"Do you find me attractive?" asked Halle

"What?!"

"I mean, under different circumstances, would you date me? I know I don't have that lusty, hot, animal look, like Kennedy. But, do I…ya know, turn men on?"

"Halle, you're like my little sister," laughed Louis. "I can't even imagine you having sex…with anyone."

"Ya know, Blake doesn't find me sexy, either."

"Well, Blake's stupid. I just feel that way 'cause I'm in love with your sister, but I'm not what she wants."

"Well, my sister's stupid. She doesn't realize how much of a good thing she's lost."

"You don't have to say that, Halle."

"I'm serious…she screwed up…but don't think this was an easy decision for her. It took her a while to decide between you and Matt. She even shed a few tears." Lou slipped into a daze. The way the moonlight shone so clearly onto the gently rippling waves of the water reminded him of the times he spent with Kennedy on the same lake.

"I never meant to hurt her. I didn't mean to make her cry," said Louis. His eyes turned red, and a single tear trickled down his cheek. Halle leaned over and pulled his head down to her chest. They both began to cry. The closer they held each other, the more the tears began to flow. Halle's hand was running up and down his back, and Louis' head was buried in her neck. Inevitably, their actions became wrapped up in a pool of emotions that erupted into lust. Louis began to slowly kiss her neck. Halle climbed onto his lap so that they were directly face to face. His hands slid down her back and under her shirt. Their bodies began to move together in an erotic dance.

Halle wanted to experience every ounce of Louis. With every fleeting passionate moment, they craved the oneness only their bodies could create. Ultimately, they were fused. She was fully accepting of every morsel of him, and he was more than willing to provide it. Their motions became more wild and animal-like with every lusty thrust. They lost all concept of time, space, and surroundings.

As their bodies moved together in a powerful and erotic dance, they accidentally knocked the car in gear. They didn't notice that the car began to roll closer and closer to the water. By the time they returned from their zone of passionate love-making, the car was half-submerged in the water. They tried to get out, but the pressure made opening the doors almost impossible. The car quickly sank, and air quickly ran out. Until their last breath, they tried to open the doors, or roll down the windows because the electrical system had shorted out.

♦

Over the next few days, a citywide search was on for Halle and Louis. By Sunday morning, their bodies were retrieved from the bottom of the lake. By Tuesday afternoon, their families had buried them. Davis was really taking this hard. He was angry and confused. He had failed at his mission and could not understand why he was nineteen years into his past if nothing would change. He snuck off to the secluded place on the lake where the crew used to hang out. It was late afternoon, and the sun was beginning to set. He sat on the bench, watching ships pass by in the distance. The sky was a weird, lavender color, and the water was grey. The red sun was setting to his left, and a mild breeze swept across the damp, dewy grass. Just then, a hand fell on his shoulder. It was Blake.

"I expected you to be out here," said Blake as he sat on the bench beside him.

"Yeah, I didn't see you at the funerals."

"That's 'cause I didn't go. I hate being sad. People spend too much time being sad and mad and angry. For all that, just be happy."

"How can you be happy when Halle and Lou are dead? And, how can you ever get true happiness when you never deal with the bad stuff? It will just sit inside you and eat you up."

"I don't expect you to jump around and sing, but we all have problems. That's the way life goes. We deal with them...then we move on. Plus, when I think that I may be the cause of Halle's death, I get about two seconds from going crazy. I don't think I can ever really and truly get over that."

"It's not your fault, Blake. It's nobody's fault. I think you should take some time for yourself to grieve and get over it. You know, if you don't face it now, you're still gonna have to face it one day."

"But, I know she wouldn't be dead if I hadn't broken up with her."

"Why did you break up with her?"

"Well, see, that's the real funny part of it all. She died without ever knowing the truth. I was kicked out of Baines for protesting, and I didn't want her to be wrapped up in this crap with Baines. But see, I found out the truth about her and Lou. They found their bodies together in your aunt's car. They were naked. See, I would have never thought that Halle was having an affair with Lou. I sacrificed my relationship with her, for her own protection, and I find out that she had been sleeping with your cousin. It's funny how things work out. I was trying to protect her from my secret, while her secret surfaces and slaps me in the face. I bet if this had happened to you, you would probably be freaking out, but you deal with shit as it happens."

"I don't think that's true, Blake. Neither Halle nor Lou was the type of person to do something like that behind your back. Lou was your family, and he wouldn't stab you in the back like that."

"You would be amazed by the things people would do. See, I'm learning new stuff everyday, and I just learned that putting all of your love into a relationship is stupid. The only person you can really depend on is yourself. I learned that it doesn't pay to have a heart because it always gets broken."

"You cannot be serious, Blake. You know, like I know, that things have a way of working themselves out. You are the most compassionate person I know. You are always looking out for the underdog and making sure everything and everybody is taken care of. I would hate to see you lose that because of some vicious rumor about two people that not only loved you, but are not able to defend themselves," explained Davis. "Like you said, shit happens...and, you deal with it. You'll love again."

"I don't think so," replied Blake somberly. "I don't think I could ever invest that much of myself into another person again--not even if I wanted to."

"Wait a minute…you said this all happened because of Baines…tell me what happened."

"See, your friend Rodney decided to tell his dad that I was involved in organizing that protest against Dr. Drew Baines for improving the school conditions."

"The school president?"

"Yeah, Rodney's dad is on the Executive Board of school affairs. He labeled me as a trouble-maker, and they expelled me."

"Did you confront Rod about this?"

"Yeah, and he gave me some bullshit story about working with the system and just doing the right thing. That brotha's got a lot of growing up to do. One day he'll see that the right thing isn't always what big brother tells you to do."

"You're right, Blake. You've been right a lot lately. Remember how you told me about how I try to plan every event in my life...?"

"Yeah, you're unprepared when things go crazy."

"I'm realizing that I can't control everything in my life. I can only do my part and be ready when things go crazy. Things change...people change...everything changes...and there's nothing anybody can do about it!" said Davis excitedly.

"Are you okay, Man?"

"Yeah, I'm fantastic! Lou's death, Paula's abortion, Kennedy's marriage, your photography—they're all things I had no control over. There is nothing me or anyone else could have done to save them."

"Photography? Davis, are you sure you're okay?"

"Yeah, Blake. I'm fine," said Davis. His tone was much calmer.

"Okay, well I gotta go," said Blake as he stood up from the bench. "Wait, I almost forgot. Did you talk to Kennedy about Paula?"

"What about her, is she okay?"

"Matt and Kennedy had to bring her to the hospital this morning. She's got some kind of infection."

"Oh, God, is she gonna be alright?"

" I don't know. You'd just better go see her."

"Alright, Blake. Thanks."

"See ya later, Man."

♦

    Davis was alone again. He looked to the now-dark purple sky and asked, "Why, Lord?" The wind grew stronger, and the air slowly became cold. Consequently, dark clouds blanketed the sky like puffs of black cotton. "You sent me back here, and I don't know what I'm doing. I have been gambling with my friends' lives, and I have been losing. All I wanted to do was go back to a place where I really knew who I was, but I've past this point in my life. Being young was nice, but living through losing my friends one time was bad enough. It was worse seeing them die again. I feel like my life is like a long, car ride. I'm looking in the rearview mirror, and I'm seeing all the people that I have loved and left behind. But, I had forgotten just how rocky that car ride was. See, what I need to do is keep my eyes on the road ahead, but I'm scared 'cause I don't know what's up there. To be honest, I don't even know what direction I'm pointed in, and I'm not even sure what my destination is."

    The wind grew even stronger and colder. The waves of the water became violent, and the mist lightly sprayed across his face. "I'm confused, and I'm scared, and I don't know what to do! I don't want a life of loneliness where my wife and child hate me. And I can't stay here and live a dead end life wondering if I'm doomed to always make the wrong choices.

    Davis stared diligently into the pool of darkness above him. "I gotta go back, Lord. I learned that there are certain things that I just cannot change, but I know I can't leave things like this. I can't help feeling some of this is my fault, and I wanna fix it. This was hell, but I would go through it again and again until I get this right. I would spend the rest of my life trying to fix their lives if I needed to. All I'm sure of is that I need to do something. I hate being here, and I don't know how to get back to where I need to be, but I don't even know where I need to be. I'm ready to go back, or forward, or whatever You got planned for me. Just as long as I'm not here!"

The purple sky cracked with a thunderous flash of light, and the violent waves made a mist that covered the land. The temperature dropped thirty degrees in two seconds, and a chill shivered through his body. At that moment, a gust of wind picked up Davis' body and flung him against a tree. The impact knocked him unconscious, and his limp body fell to the cold, wet grass.

He awoke to the sound of persistent knocking. The room was dark, and Davis was disoriented. He blindly followed the knocking to the window. Outside, stood a nineteen-year-old Rodney wearing green jeans and a green-and-white striped shirt.

"Y-y-you ready to go?" he asked.

Davis wiped his eyes to make sure he was seeing what he thought he was seeing. He took a deep breath and muttered one word, "Damn!"

The End
■

Printed in the United States
49829LVS00004B/86